Adventures with Psalmy

Christine Smith McClure

This book is written by Mrs. Christine Smith McClure and dedicated to her Mom who has always encouraged her to write her stories down to be read and enjoyed by others.

It was a beautiful day on the Dreams Hope and Faith Ranch. I had been just awakened by the rattling of the feed bucket. At first I clumsily get up but then I race to the fence line to meet my owner. I knicker and he calls back, "come on ole boy." He is the nicest guy ever. I really love him because he always has such great things to say to me and extra treats. I can hardly wait for him to dump some delicious food over the fence. I

prance back and forth in anticipation.

I am so excited because I love to eat.

I can remember my first drink of my

momma's milk to my first bite of

grain.

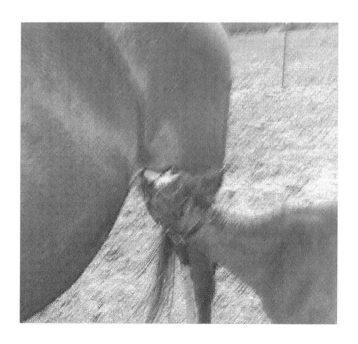

Finally, my favorite person tossed the feed over the fence and I drop my head to eat this glorious molasses covered grain. It is as sweet as candy. I know about candy because my owner allows me to have real candy that he makes. That is right, he makes it homemade. It is a cinnamon flavor and is so good. He calls it hard tack candy. I misheard him the first time he brought it to me and I thought he said, "Here Psalmy, is some heart attack candy." This confused me a little because my owner would never do anything to hurt me. So I listened in as he gently offered me another piece with his hand opened wide and flat so that I could get a bite. He said, "Hmm, Psalm I thought you would like hard tack candy." As soon as I could believe my ears I eagerly took the piece of candy and crunched it up and swallowed it.

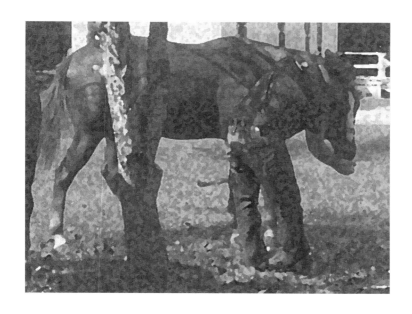

Here at Dreams Hope and Faith Ranch we have some more horse friends and a great orchard with fruit trees. By the way did I tell you how much I love pears? I love, love, love pears.

They are so sweet and I sneak extra every time I get to go to the pasture. My lady owner is pretty swell too. She doesn't let me have as many treats as the man but she sure teaches me all kinds of stuff. She teaches me how to do this thing called lunging. She gets this really long rope and sends me out on the end of it and I listen for her to give me commands. She tells me to walk.

That is the slowest I go and I am not that fond of it. I like to move out. She usually transitions me into the jog/ trot next. I am really good at this as I have long legs and look like I am floating across the ground with my flaxen mane and tail. I am what is called a red sorrel color. People just love my movement and my pretty mane and tail. Sometimes I accidently break into a lope/ canter.

I don't mean to it is just that I love to move and move fast. My lady owner slows me down with verbal cues and she gently tugs on the rope that is connected to my halter. She also slightly bends forward and I know I need to slow my speed to the gait she says.

I just love it here at Dreams, Hope and Faith Ranch. My life is perfect I have plenty to eat, lots of friends and the coolest owners. They say I am pretty curious. Whatever that means! If that means I like to get into stuff, then yes I am CURIOUS! It is just my investigative nature to explore. I like to experience things with all my senses especially, my mouth. So just have to share with you, my man owner, whom I especially adore, left his rubber boots near my paddock. I found them interesting and decided to pick them up and try them on. This might sound absolutely silly to you but, I figure if he can wear them so can I. I carefully arched my neck just right so that I could reach down and grab them without getting bit by the electric fence. That thing hurts. You wouldn't think that wire would sting so much but wow, it can make your head spin. So I am standing there with a rubber boot in my mouth just a swinging it round and round trying to get my foot in with no luck. I see that male owner of mine just a laughing at me. He thinks it is funny I can't get the boot on. The lady kind gives me a, "what in the world are you doing" look. Just to keep that guy laughing I just continue to stand perfectly still and swing the boot in circles.

One hot July morning my best friend Mr. Steve comes out to greet me. Yes my man owner's name is Mr. Steve. He has a bright red lead rope in hand and snaps it on my halter. I willingly walk alongside him. I think this is the most respective way I can go. I think that going on in front of him would be rude.

Lagging behind would probably make him think I am uninterested in the new adventure that might be around the corner. So yes, alongside, stride in stride we walk together to this thing

he calls a horse trailer. He tells me

how I can be calm and just step on

this thing with wheels. He also says he

has a special surprise for me. I love

surprises so I step on the trailer. He

gives me a treat because I do a great

job of just stepping up on this

contraption. Just then he shuts the

door and I hear that truck of theirs

start up. Wait, I think to myself,,, the

truck is hooked to this trailer. I must

be going somewhere. After a short

ride I feel the trailer coming to a

stop. There he is again, telling me

Psalmy it is time to get off. I am not

quite sure about this as I tend to

easily get into things but need a little

coaxing to get myself out of

predicaments. He pleads with me

but, I just stand there. Then my lady

Mrs. Christine, uses her soothing

voice and gently tells me to back. I do it because I completely trust her. I hear her tell me to back and then to step down, followed up with, "good boy." To my surprise, we are at a river. Oh, how I love water and splashing in my trough at home. I can hardly wait to try it in the big river. This is going to be a great adventure. I hear my owners talking about how they are not sure how I will take to water and to be careful. Mr. Steve walks in the river and gently pulls the

rope to ask me to come in too. I

take a big breath and walk in. It is

cold. It is also hot outside so I

welcome the coolness on my body.

Mr. Steve takes me deeper and

deeper. This is so fun, what an

adventure.

Wow, what a day! I got to go

swimming. This is way cool, I can't

wait to tell the other horses at the

Ranch. So I eagerly jump on the

trailer and stand just right while they

swing the door closed behind me. On

the ride home I begin to get a little sleepy as it hard work to go swimming. I wish I could lay down. Maybe when I get home I can lay down and rest. However, until I get home I am going to stand here and doze. I don't know why but my knees lock when I am sleeping and it allows me to sleep while standing. My Mommy Reiner told me this when I was super young. She was a great

Mom, she taught me everything I needed to know up until Mr. Steve and Mrs. Christine came to our home and doted over me commenting on how well put together I was and how my curious temperament would make me a great horse. I wanted to go home with them right then and there but they waited a while and one day finally came back to my home and told my owners they would like to have me.

Well that ride was short. Here we

are back at the Ranch. Whew, I can

not wait to get that nap in where I

can lay down and really catch some

zzs.

Here I am plopped down in the Mr.

Steve and Mrs. Christine's front

yard. They put up temporary fence

for me to eat all the sweet grass.

Well by now you know I love food.

So not much better to eat than sweet

tender grass. But then again I love

grain, pears, apples, pears, hay, and CANDY! Something else I love is Sweet Tea! Oh my, it is ever so good. I had my first taste from Mr. Steve and love it anytime he allows me to have some.

Well that is all for now folks! Catch

me on another adventure soon!

Meet the Author:

Mrs. Christine Smith McClure lives

In South Carolina on Dreams Hope &

Faith Ranch where she and her

Husband raise quarter horses.

She is an Elementary teacher and

loves everything horses.

Psalmy is up for almost anything!

Here he takes a sniff of roses

followed by a big bite full.

Psalmy decided to try his hooves at

dancing as this is a dance floor my

husband built for a wedding held here

at Dreams Hope &Faith Ranch.

Be sure to follow Author Christine Smith McClure on Facebook. Learn about new books that she is writing, book signings and readings. Author Christine Smith McClure astride her horse FQH Blue Delux. Christine writes for all ages and genres. She especially enjoys writing children's books about her favorite subject none other than the horse. She is a lady of many talents. She is an avid member of the horse community where she works with her horses, shows, and promotes the industry. She and her husband live on and run Dreams Hope & Faith Ranch in South Carolina where they raise quarter horses. When not writing or riding she enjoys spending time with family, cooking and creating art. She is an educator by profession and is currently teaching second grade.

Made in the USA
Columbia, SC
24 September 2024

42248354R00019